AN ANACONDA ATE MY HOMEWORK!

By Alice Schertle
Pictures by Aaron Renier

Disney · HYPERION BOOKS
New York

To Spence, Dylan, Jen, Drew, Kate, and John —AS

Welcome to the world, Axel Oliver! —AR

Text copyright © 2009 by Alice Schertle
Illustrations © 2009 by Aaron Renier
Colors by Alec Longstreth

First Edition
10 9 8 7 6 5 4 3 2 1
Printed in Singapore
Reinforced binding
ISBN 978-1-4231-1354-6
Library of Congress Cataloging-in-Publication Data on file

Visit www.hyperionbooksforchildren.com

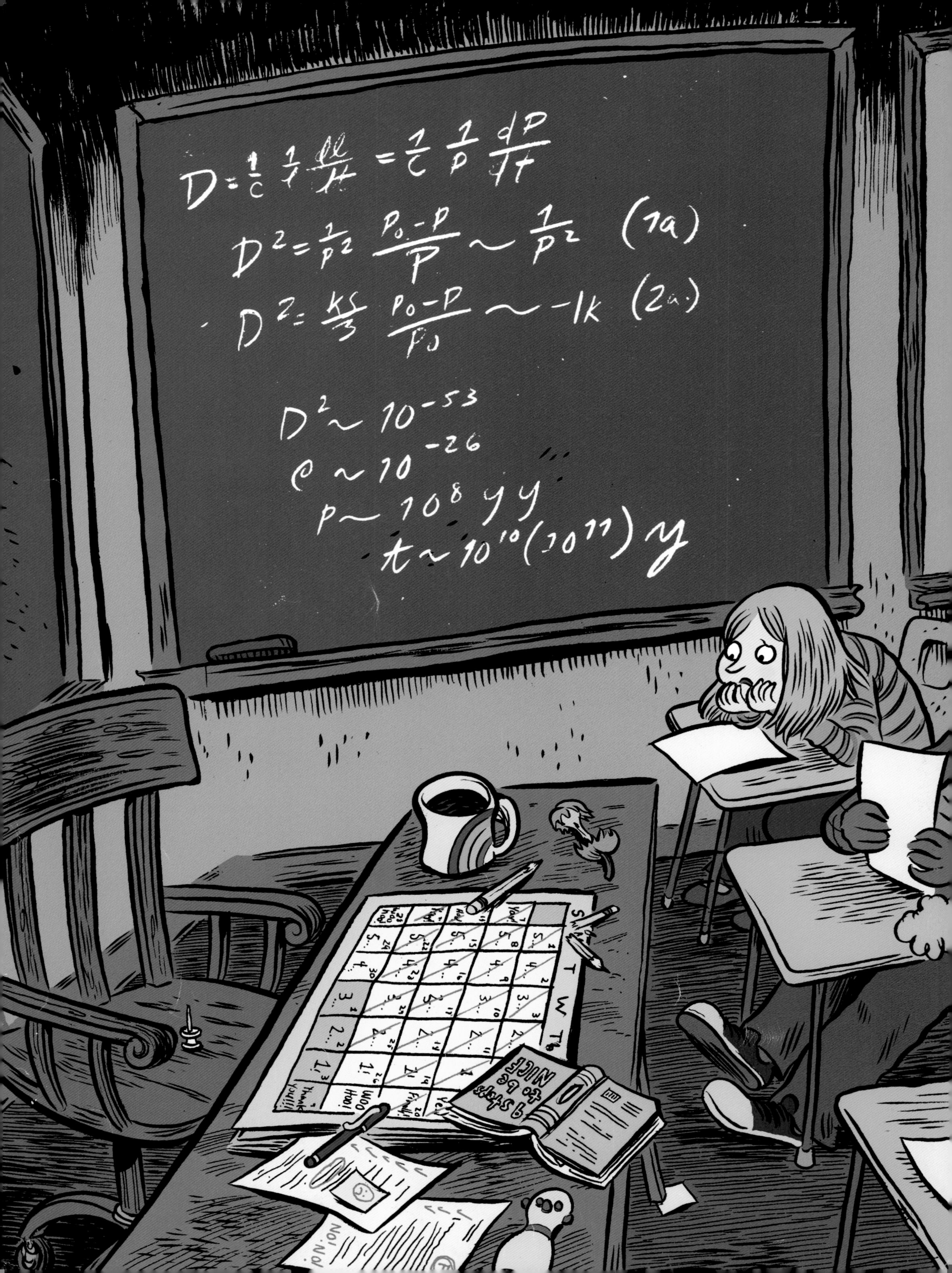

(1a)
(2a)
9 Steps to be NICE

School was almost out for the day. In Digby's classroom Mr. Crumbundle, known to some as Crummy, passed out homework assignments.

Digby stuffed the papers into his backpack and started off for home.

But, as luck would have it, when Digby turned the corner . . .

a Gigantic Repulsive Raptor swooped out of the sky.

Luckily, Digby always carried a wad of already-been-chewed bubble gum in his backpack.
Some for you... and some for ME!
POP!
Good thing it's DOUBLE-STRENGTH MUSCLE BUBBLE....

Digby kept his head. . . .

As luck would have it, the crocodiles had just eaten a small rowboat and weren't hungry.

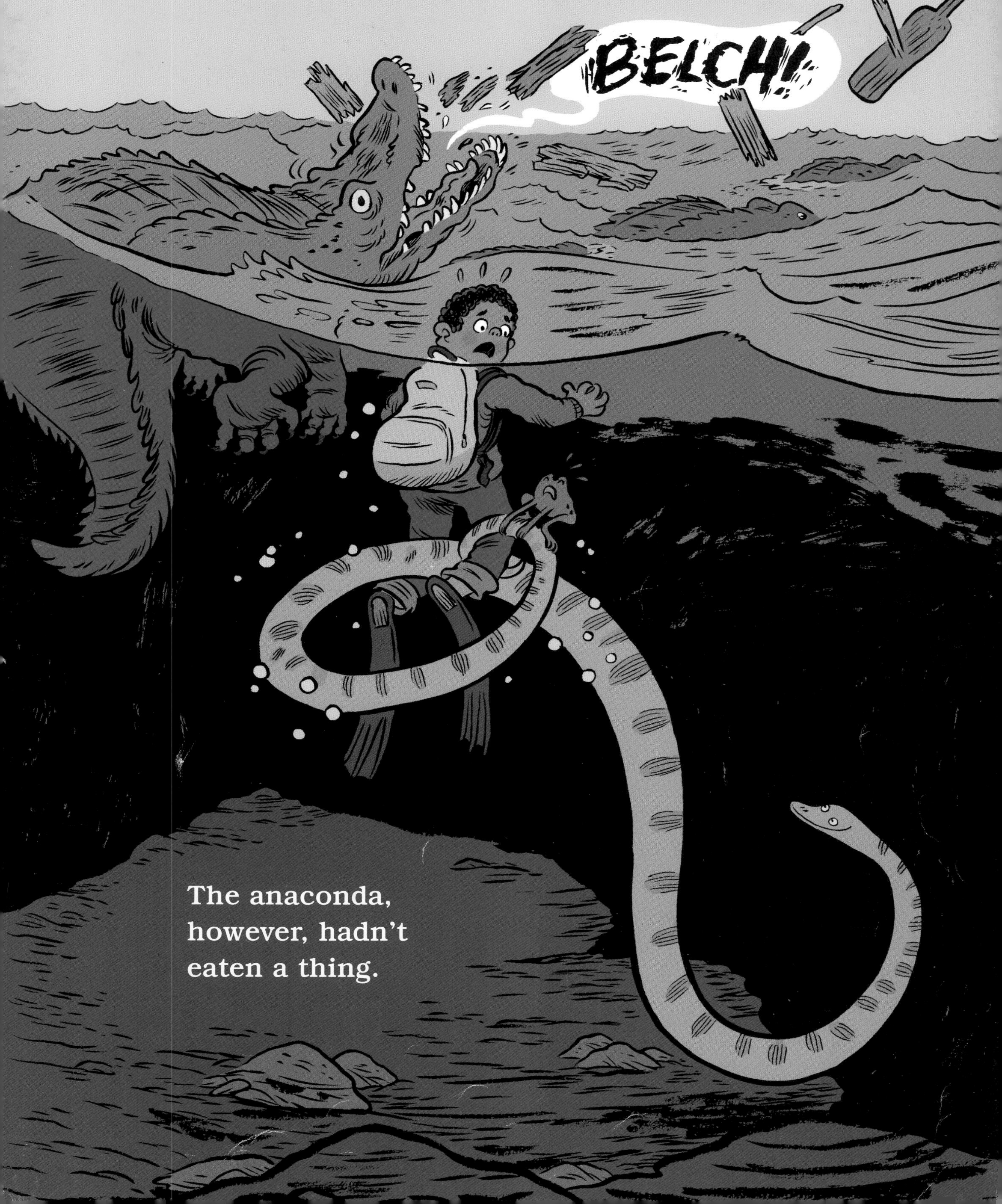

The anaconda, however, hadn't eaten a thing.

I'M A KID. A KID INSIDE A SNAKE. NO CRACKERS, THANKS.

Not a talkin' snake.

Just a dumb kid.

Luckily, Digby carried a complete line of party balloons in his backpack. . . .

He would have had a nasty fall had it not been for the large hand that reached out from the underbrush and held him up.

While the gorilla crashed through the jungle to retrieve the ball, Digby took the opportunity to jog off down the path.

The tiger had never had a breath
freshener before. When it clamped
its mouth shut, Digby scrambled
up a nearby trunk.

As luck would have it . . .

. . . it was not a *tree* trunk.

Sitting on the head of an enormous rogue elephant, Digby kept his head.

SNACK TIME!

MNCH! MNCH!

Digby and the elephant soon became fast friends.

Meanwhile, in a small clearing, members of the OHNO television news network were scouting the jungle for breaking news.

OHNO 1

Seeing Digby and the rogue elephant, they sensed a story. Digby would be on the evening news!

He was flown back to civilization . . .

When the story was over, the president wanted to see what else was in Digby's backpack.

As luck would have it, she *loved* story time.

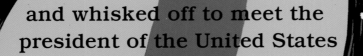

and whisked off to meet the president of the United States

to tell her the story of his adventure.

The president picked up a pen and wrote across the top of every page.

She gave Digby the presidential pen to keep in his backpack.
CLICK CLICK
The next day at school, Mr. Crumbundle, known to some as Crummy, collected the homework and read the president's notes.
The... P-P-Pres...

He fainted dead away and later had to be taken to the nurse's office for a shot.

School was dismissed for the day.

Digby hitched up his backpack, in which he carried a few essentials.

As he rounded the corner, he saw, leering down at him from a height of twenty feet, a Humongous, Red-Eyed, Smelly-Toed, Yellow-Fanged—

But as luck would have it, this is . . .